THE ADVENTURES OF BADDU AND CHHOTU

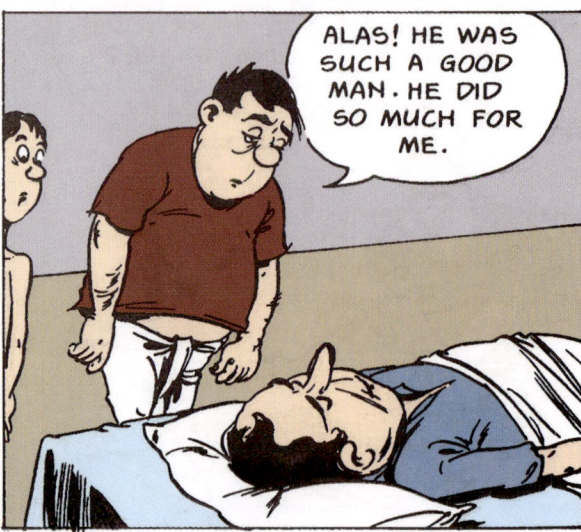

Suppandi and his friends are all packed!

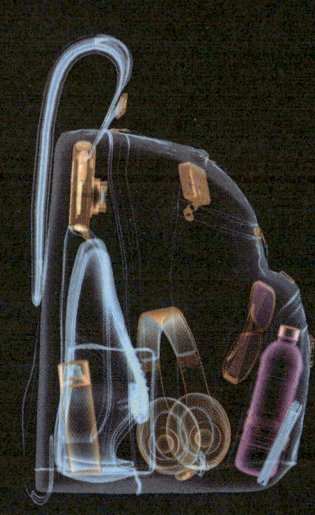

This time your favourite characters are bringing their (mis)adventures to your holiday. ACK Media introduces its special travel collection of Tinkle Digests, Amar Chitra Katha comics and Karadi Tales picture books (for the younger globetrotters), to make your travels more fun.

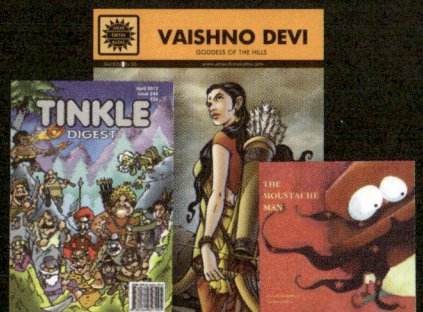

www.amarchitrakatha.com

Make sure you're packed. Log on to our website now to buy any comic or picture book with your special 25%* discount code: 'NGT 25', and have your favourite travel companions delivered straight to your doorstep.

A COLLECTOR'S EDITION, FROM INDIA'S FAVOURITE STORYTELLER.

India's greatest epic, told over 1,300 beautifully illustrated pages. The Mahabharata Collector's Edition. It's not just a set of books, it's a piece of culture.

THE MAHABHARATA
COLLECTOR'S EDITION
Rupees one thousand, nine hundred and ninety-nine only.

BIKAL THE TERRIBLE
THE TALE OF A FRIGHTENED TIGER

The route to your roots

BIKAL THE TERRIBLE

Bikal is the original 'He-Who-Must-Not-Be-Named'. The best way to ward off Bikal the Terrible is to avoid taking his name. The word Bikal inspires such fear and awe that even a tiger gets scared of Bikal and tamely allows himself to be fooled by two daredevils. This is a delightful folktale from Madhya Pradesh.

Script
Meera Ugra and
and Luis Fernandes

Illustrations
Dilip Kadam

Editor
Anant Pai

* A WORD USED BY THE TRIBALS FOR THAT WHICH IS TO BE FEARED, IN THIS CASE THE PROWLING TIGER.

IT'S PITCH-DARK IN THERE.
ALL THE BETTER FOR US.
SOON —
I THINK IT'S A BULLOCK. BUT THERE'S NO CART.
WE LL PUT THE SACKS ON HIS BACK.
WHILE THEY TALKED THE TIGER WAS FAST ASLEEP...
...AND IN THE MIDST OF A NIGHTMARE.
HELP! BIKAL HAS CAUGHT ME!

AS THE LOOT WAS LOADED ON HIS BACK—
WHA-AT!
NO ORDINARY MAN WOULD DARE TREAT ME SO. MY WORST FEARS HAVE COME TRUE!
I AM IN THE CLUTCHES OF THE TERRIBLE BIKAL AND HIS FRIENDS!
OOOOH! THE LOAD IS HEAVY. BUT I DARE NOT PROTEST.
WE ARE RICH MEN NOW. I'LL BUY AS MANY GOATS AS I CAN WITH MY SHARE.
I'LL BUY SOME LAND.
AS FOR ME, I WILL GET MARRIED.

I-I WONDER WHAT WILL HAPPEN TO ME.
AT DAWN —
THERE'S ENOUGH LIGHT TO SEE WHAT WE HAVE. LET'S DIVIDE THE LOOT.
YES, I WOULD LIKE TO BUY THE GOATS AS SOON A-AS...!
F-FRIENDS, AM I DREAMING?
N-NO...
IT'S A... IT'S A...
TIGER!

OH, WHAT A FOOL I HAVE MADE OF MYSELF ! THEY WERE JUST MEN — ORDINARY MEN !
EVERYONE WILL LAUGH AT ME IF THEY COME TO HEAR OF THIS.
AS HE WAS WANDERING AROUND, FEELING RATHER ASHAMED OF HIMSELF, THE BUNDLE ON HIS BACK GOT CAUGHT BETWEEN TWO ROCKS.
OOOF! NOW HOW DO I GET OUT ?
JUST THEN HE SPOTTED A COWHERD.
O COWHERD...
DON'T RUN AWAY. I WON'T EAT YOU.
IT'S BIKAL!
PLEASE COME BACK. SOMEBODY HAS TIED THIS SACK ON MY BACK. PLEASE TAKE IT DOWN. I SWEAR I WON'T HARM YOU.

THE SACK IS FULL OF MONEY. YOU CAN HAVE ALL OF IT.
MONEY!
YOU PROMISE NOT TO HURT ME?
I PROMISE.
TELL ME, HOW DID THIS HAPPEN?
IT'S ALL BECAUSE OF THAT BIKAL!
THE COWHERD WAS PUZZLED.
BUT... BUT... YOU ARE A... HOW COULD BIKAL...
NEVER UTTER THAT WORD AGAIN, DO YOU HEAR? I HATE THE SOUND OF IT.

DON'T GET ANGRY. I–I'LL NEVER UTTER THAT NAME AGAIN.
IF YOU DO I'LL COME AND DEVOUR YOU. NOW YOU MAY GO.
THE COWHERD RUSHED HOME WITH THE LOOT.
WHAT A STROKE OF LUCK! I HAVE SUDDENLY BECOME A RICH MAN!
MONTHS PASSED. HE BOUGHT COWS AND BUFFALOES...
...AND MARRIED BHAGWATI, THE MOST INTELLIGENT, HARD-WORKING GIRL IN THE VILLAGE.
ONE NIGHT—
SHAMBHU, HOW DID YOU BECOME SO RICH?
IT'S A LONG STORY, BHAGO. THERE WAS THIS BIKAL...
AS SHAMBHU FINISHED NARRATING THE STORY, THE TIGER HAPPENED TO STROLL BY.

IT'S THE COWHERD WHO HELPED ME! I'LL GO AND MEET HIM.
SHAMBHU, I FEEL LIKE GOING TO MY PARENT'S HOUSE.
NOW? AT THIS HOUR?
AREN'T YOU AFRAID OF BIKAL?
GRR-RRR! HE HAS UTTERED THE FORBIDDEN WORD.
I WON'T SPARE HIM NOW.
LET'S GO TOMORROW MORNING, BHAGO.
OH, ALL RIGHT.
LATER THAT NIGHT THE TIGER CREPT INTO THE HOUSE ...

| ...STEALTHILY LIFTED THE SLEEPING SHAMBHU... | ...AND LEFT WITHOUT DISTURBING BHAGWATI. |

HE CARRIED THE COWHERD TO THE FOREST. THERE, HE THREW HIM DOWN WITH A THUD.

OW! WHERE AM I? WHAT HAPPENED?

OH! IT'S YOU...

YES, YOU BROKE YOUR PROMISE SO I AM GOING TO EAT YOU.

WAIT! EAT ME BY ALL MEANS BUT IN THE MORNING.

WHY NOT NOW?

MY FLESH IS TOUGH NOW BECAUSE OF THE COLD, BUT IT WILL BECOME TENDER AND WARM WITH THE MORNING SUN.

JUST THINK IT OVER! TO ME IT'S ALL THE SAME WHETHER YOU EAT ME NOW OR A FEW HOURS LATER. BUT TO YOU, IT WOULD MEAN A TASTIER MEAL.
ALL RIGHT, WE'LL WAIT.
I HAVE GAINED TIME. NOW LET'S HOPE BHAGO NOTICES MY ABSENCE AND ARRANGES FOR MY RESCUE.
MEANWHILE BHAGWATI HAD INDEED DISCOVERED HER HUSBAND'S ABSENCE.
WHERE HAS HE GONE?
WHAT'S THIS?
HAS A TIGER CARRIED HIM AWAY? IF THAT'S THE CASE, I'LL HAVE TO ACT QUICKLY TO SAVE HIM.
SHE THOUGHT OF A PLAN AND SET TO WORK ON IT.
...I'LL ALSO NEED A CUDGEL AND A DRUM TO FRIGHTEN THE WILD ANIMALS...

SOMETIME LATER, THE TIGER, WHO WAS PATIENTLY WAITING FOR THE SUN TO RISE, HEARD A WEIRD SOUND.

THAK CHHANNAN CHHANN DHAM

CHOOM CHOOM CHOOM CHOOM

WH...WHAT'S THAT?

DRUMBEATS! THE SOUND OF ANKLETS! COULD IT BE BHAGO?

I AM SURE IT IS!

WHY DON'T YOU ANSWER? IS IT...IS IT...B...BIKAL?

THAK CHHANNAN THAK DHAK

I MUST LET HER KNOW I'M HERE.

ANSWER ME! IS IT BIKAL?

YES, IT IS BIKAL!
THAT WAS MY HUSBAND'S VOICE! HE'S ALIVE!
THERE HE IS! ...OH, THE TIGER IS WITH HIM TOO.
THE TIGER THINKS I AM BIKAL! AND HE'S TERRIFIED! GOOD! I'LL PLAY UPON THAT!
WHO'S THERE? ARE THERE ANY TIGERS AROUND FOR ME TO EAT?
HE'S LOOKING FOR TIGERS TO EAT! WHAT SHOULD I DO?
HOW SHOULD I KNOW?

AHA! I CAN SMELL A TIGER!
PLEASE HELP ME. IF YOU DO, I WON'T EAT YOU.
WELL...I'LL TRY. JUST LIE DOWN AND KEEP STILL.
SPEAK UP! HAVE YOU SEEN ANY TIGERS WHICH I CAN EAT?
NO, THERE AREN'T ANY HERE. GO AWAY!
THEN WHAT'S THAT NEXT TO YOU?
THIS? OH— IT'S JUST A PILE OF DIRTY CLOTHES.
REALLY? I DON'T BELIEVE YOU! HIT THE PILE WITH A ROCK.

AS SHAMBHU HESITATED —
FRIEND, DO HIT ME ... YOU MUST DO WHAT BIKAL SAYS IN ORDER TO SAVE ME.
BUT HIT ME GENTLY...
THE COWHERD HIT THE TIGER GENTLY ON THE HEAD. THEN —
HIT IT HARDER IF IT IS MERELY A PILE OF CLOTHES.
YES. HIT A LITTLE HARDER OTHERWISE...
THIS WENT ON FOR A WHILE.
HARDER! HARDER!
YES, A LITTLE HARDER...
AFTER A WHILE —
HARDER...
NO NEED DEAR, OUR FRIEND HAS SWOONED.
LEAVING THE WOUNDED TIGER TO ITS FATE THE CLEVER COUPLE HAPPILY RETURNED HOME.

THE TIGER-TAMERS
TWO MISCHIEVOUS BOYS ONCE LIVED IN A VILLAGE.
THEY DIDN'T DO A SPOT OF WORK BUT ALL THE TIME HARASSED THOSE WHO DID.
HERE THEY COME NOW. GET READY.
TAKE AIM.
SHOOT!
THACK
EEEEEK!

HAHAHAHA!
IT'S THOSE TWO RASCALS AGAIN.
YOU...YOU DEVILS!
I'LL BEAT YOUR BRAINS OUT!
HAHAHA! HA HA HA!
WHEN THEY WERE NOT SHOOTING AT WATERPOTS THEY WOULD BE SHOOTING AT CHICKENS.
CACKCACKCACK!
MY CHICKENS.
ONE DAY—
LET'S DRIVE THOSE GOATS AWAY.
YES. IT'LL BE GREAT FUN.
SHOOO!
SHOOO!

MY GOATS! MY GOATS!
THOSE BOYS ARE DRIVING AWAY MY GOATS!
THEY ARE BECOMING BOLDER AND BOLDER.
LET'S CATCH THEM AND GIVE THEM A GOOD THRASHING. COME ON!
THEY'RE COMING AFTER US. RUN!
THE BOYS ABANDONED THE GOATS AND TOOK OFF IN ANOTHER DIRECTION.
FOLLOW ME!

"AFTER THEM! WE SHOULDN'T LET THEM GO THIS TIME!"

"LET'S HEAD FOR THE JUNGLE."

"CATCH THEM! CATCH THEM!"

BUT THE BOYS OUTRAN THE VILLAGERS...

...AND KEPT RUNNING TILL THEY REACHED THE SAFETY OF THE JUNGLE.

THERE, EXHAUSTED, THEY THREW THEMSELVES ON THE GROUND.

"PHEW!" "HAH!"

WHEN THEY HAD RECOVERED THEIR BREATH SOMEWHAT—

"NOW WHERE DO WE GO FROM HERE?" "WE CAN ONLY GO FORWARD."

"YOU ARE RIGHT. IT'LL TAKE SOME DAYS FOR THOSE PEOPLE TO COOL DOWN...IF AT ALL THEY DO COOL DOWN."

SO THE BOYS WENT DEEPER INTO THE JUNGLE.

THEY WALKED ON AND ON, THEN STOPPED DEAD...

...FOR SEATED IN THE MIDDLE OF THEIR PATH WAS AN ENORMOUS TIGER.

THE YOUNGER BOY SUDDENLY DARTED FORWARD...

...THREW HIMSELF ON THE TIGER'S BACK...

...AND CATCHING HOLD OF THE ANIMAL'S EARS PUSHED HIS HEAD DOWN. AT THE SAME TIME THE OLDER BOY GRABBED HIS TAIL.

GOT YOU!

THE TIGER WAS STARTLED OUT OF HIS WITS.
ARRGH! WHAT'S HAPPENING? WHO HAS CAUGHT ME?
W-WHO ARE YOU? WHAT DO YOU WANT WITH ME?
WE ARE TIGER-HUNTERS.
WE NEED A TIGER TO PULL OUR PLOUGH.
YOU USE TIGERS TO PULL YOUR PLOUGH!
THERE MUST BE SOME MISTAKE. WHAT YOU NEED IS A PAIR OF BULLOCKS.
WHEN YOU PLOUGH WITH BULLOCKS YOU GET ONLY RICE AND SUCH CROPS...
...BUT WHEN YOU PLOUGH WITH TIGERS YOU GET GOLD AND SILVER.
IS-IS THAT SO?
WE HAVE ALREADY CAUGHT ONE TIGER, YOU ARE THE SECOND ONE.
THIS IS TERRIBLE.

LET'S SHOW HIM THE TIGER WE'VE ALREADY CAUGHT!
IF THEY'VE CAUGHT SUCH A NASTY-LOOKING FELLOW WHAT CHANCE HAVE I OF ESCAPING?
WHAT SHALL I DO? IF I DO ESCAPE, I'LL FEED A DOZEN TIGERS! OH! IF ONLY I COULD...

BIKAL THE TERRIBLE

"LOOK FRIENDS, IF IT'S GOLD AND SILVER YOU ARE AFTER, I CAN GIVE YOU HEAPS OF IT."

"I HAVE KILLED AND EATEN SEVERAL PRINCES AND KINGS IN MY LIFETIME AND ALL THEIR GOLD IS LYING AROUND IN MY CAVE. I'LL BRING IT FOR YOU."

"HOW DO WE KNOW THAT YOU AREN'T MAKING IT ALL UP JUST TO ESCAPE?"

"YES, HOW DO WE KNOW?"

"COME WITH ME TO MY CAVE IF YOU DON'T BELIEVE ME."

THE TIGER, TREMBLING WITH FEAR, LED THE BOYS TO HIS CAVE.

THIS IS WHERE I LIVE. NOW PLEASE LET ME...

IF THEY THINK I AM GOING TO WAIT FOR THEM, THEY ARE MISTAKEN.

THE TIGER RAN AND RAN...

...TILL HE HAD LEFT THE CAVE AND THE BOYS FAR BEHIND.

THAT WAS A NARROW ESCAPE! BUT FOR MY QUICK THINKING I WOULD HAVE ENDED UP YOKED TO A PLOUGH FOR THE REST OF MY LIFE.

"NOW TO FEED THE TWELVE TIGERS."

HE STALKED...

...AND KILLED A SAMBHAR...

...AND WENT TO INVITE HIS FRIENDS TO EAT WITH HIM.

MEANWHILE INSIDE HIS CAVE —

"NECKLACES! ARMLETS! CROWNS!"

"HE WAS NOT EXAGGERATING ABOUT THE WEALTH HERE."

THE TWO BOYS GATHERED TOGETHER ALL THE ORNAMENTS LYING IN AND AROUND THE CAVE...

...AND NOT FINDING THE TIGER OUTSIDE...

...WENT ON THEIR WAY.
AS THEY WALKED ON—
ARE WE GOING TOWARDS THE VILLAGE OR AWAY FROM IT ?
I DON'T KNOW.
I THINK WE ARE LOST. TRY TO REMEMBER WHICH WAY WE CAME... WHAT ARE YOU STARING AT ?
TIGERS!
TEN — TWELVE — THIRTEEN OF THEM...
WE'RE DONE FOR IF THEY SEE US!
LET'S CLIMB UP THAT TREE.

FASTER!
ONE OF THE BOYS MANAGED TO SCRAMBLE ONTO A BRANCH...
... BUT THE OTHER WAS A LITTLE SLOW AND HE WAS STILL HALF-WAY UP THE TRUNK WHEN THE TIGERS CAME INTO VIEW.
I'D BETTER STAY WHERE I AM. IF I MOVE, IT'LL ATTRACT THEIR ATTENTION.
HERE IS THE SAMBHAR, MY FRIENDS.
WE'LL DRAG IT TO THAT TREE AND EAT IT THERE.

OH, NO! THEY ARE COMING HERE.

OOOO-H! MY ARMS... I...I CAN'T HANG ON MUCH LONGER.

THE TIGERS MADE THEMSELVES COMFORTABLE UNDER THE TREE. THEN THE OLDEST AMONG THEM TURNED TO THE HOST.

NOW BEFORE WE START, PLEASE TELL US WHY YOU ARE FEASTING US.

ER... WELL...

LET'S SAY, IT'S TO CELEBRATE MY NARROW ESCAPE.

NARROW ESCAPE?

YES. THIS AFTERNOON I WAS SEIZED BY TWO MONSTERS. SUCH FIENDISH CREATURES YOU COULD NEVER HAVE SEEN BEFORE!

THEY NEEDED TWO TIGERS TO PULL THEIR PLOUGH AND THEY HAD ALREADY CAUGHT ONE. THEY WERE ALL SET TO TAKE ME AWAY TOO.

YOU DON'T SAY!

HOW DID YOU ESCAPE?
I USED MY BRAINS...
I SAID TO THEM...!!
YEOOO E W!
?!
?!
OH, MY GOD!
?!
THUMP
GRAB THE OLD TIGER! DON'T LET HIM GET AWAY!
GRAB HIM!
IT'S THEM!
WHAT!
MY FRIENDS, IT'S THOSE TWO MONSTERS I WAS TELLING YOU ABOUT!

"RUN! RUN FOR YOUR LIVES!"

SHAKEN TO THE CORE, THE TIGERS LEAPED OVER EACH OTHER AND FLED IN TERROR.

"GOOD THINKING, BROTHER. I THOUGHT IT WAS THE END FOR ME."

"ANYWAY, WHILE I WAS UP THERE I SAW THE ROUTE WE SHOULD TAKE TO GET BACK TO OUR VILLAGE."

"SO LET'S GO BACK HOME. THOSE PEOPLE ARE SURE TO FORGIVE US WHEN THEY HEAR ABOUT OUR ADVENTURE AND SEE WHAT WE HAVE IN OUR BUNDLE."

BEGINNING OF AN EPIC SAGA
BALA KAND

AMAR CHITRA KATHA

The divine story of Rama's birth

His heroic adventures with Lakshmana

The stirring legend of Shiva's bow

Amar Chitra Katha presents the seven kands of Valmiki's Ramayana.

Start your collection now!

AMAR CHITRA KATHA

3-IN-1

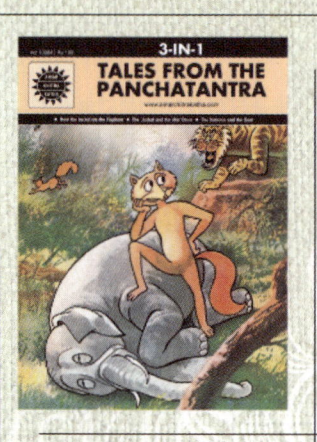

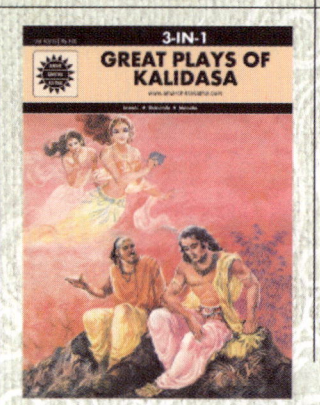

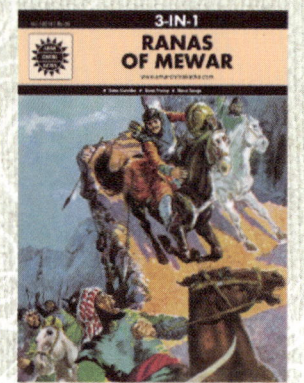

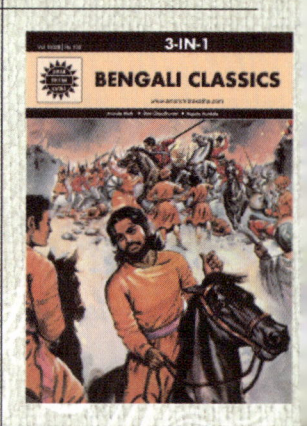

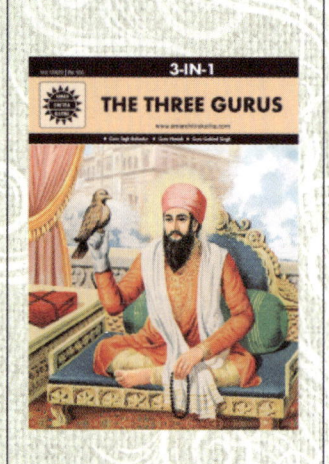

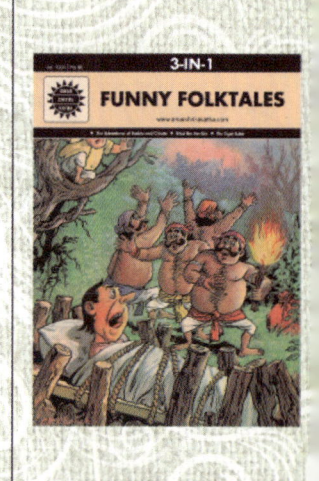

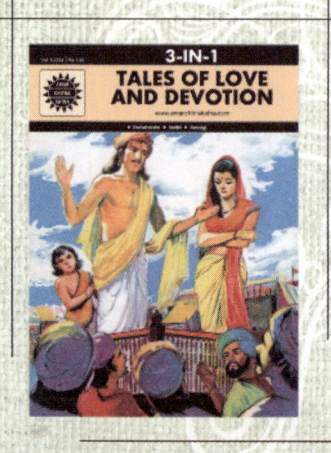

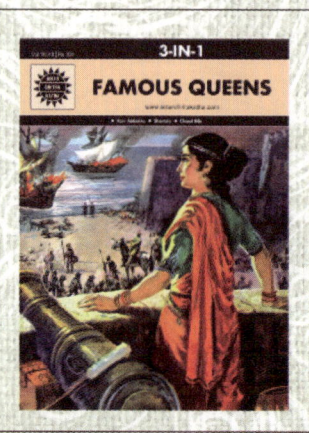

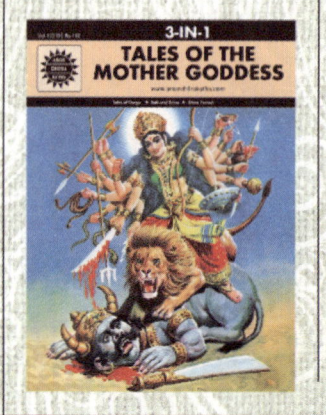

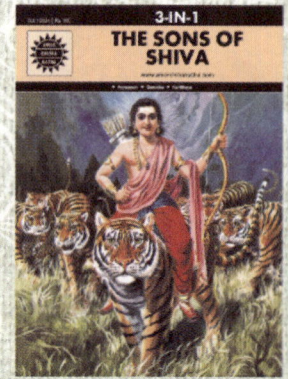

- TALES FROM THE PANCHATANTRA
- GREAT PLAYS OF KALIDASA
- RANAS OF MEWAR
- BENGALI CLASSICS
- THE THREE GURUS
- FUNNY FOLKTALES
- TALES OF LOVE AND DEVOTION
- FAMOUS QUEENS
- TALES OF THE MOTHER GODDESS
- THE SONS OF SHIVA

Over 50 titles available in paperback

All titles available on www.amarchitrakatha.com.

THE TIGER-EATER

BRAIN BEATS BRAWN

The route to your roots

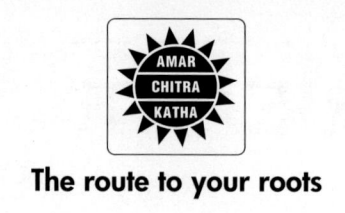

THE TIGER-EATER

Packed with laughs, these tales from Punjab teach as they entertain. They also present a quirky view of a world where idleness is an art, a devious mind a cherished talent, and humour the ultimate virtue. As animals pit their might against men and women, we are assured, happily, that the brain is mightier than mere brawn.

Script	Illustrations	Editor
Subba Rao	Ram Waeerkar	Anant Pai

THE TIGER-EATER

SHERSINGH WAS PLOUGHING HIS FIELD WHEN...

...A TIGER QUIETLY WALKED UP TO HIM.

GOOD MORNING, FRIEND. HAVE YOU HAD YOUR BREAKFAST?

Y...ES!

THEN I WILL HAVE MINE.

PLEASE UNYOKE THOSE BULLOCKS.

NO! NO!

YOU CAN'T EAT MY BULLOCKS!

AND WHY NOT?

YOU'VE HAD A GOOD BREAKFAST, AND YOU EXPECT ME TO STARVE!
UNYOKE THOSE BULLOCKS!
I MUST SAVE MY BULLOCKS AT ANY COST!
MY LORD! SPARE THE BULLOCKS. YOU CAN HAVE THE COW MY WIFE LOOKS AFTER.
OH, WELL. ONE ANIMAL IS AS GOOD AS ANOTHER. ALL RIGHT, I'LL SETTLE FOR THE COW.
BUT DON'T TRY ANY TRICKS.
I WOULDN'T DARE, MY LORD. I'LL SEND MY WIFE WITH THE COW.

THE TIGER EATER

When Shersingh reached home —

"Is that you?"

"Yes! We're in trouble! Real trouble!"

When Shersingh told her all about the tiger —

"And you want to save your bullocks at the cost of my cow!"

"We could live without milk but not without bread. And where will the bread come from without corn?"

"How can I grow corn without ploughing the fields? And how can I plough without my bullocks?"

"You see I have reasoned it out and..."

"Yet couldn't outsmart a stupid tiger."

"You need a brain for that."

GO TO THE TIGER AND TELL HIM I AM BRINGING THE COW.
YOU WANT ME TO GO BACK TO THE TIGER?
CAN'T YOU GIVE A SIMPLE MESSAGE TO A STUPID ANIMAL?
SHERSINGH LEFT WITHOUT FURTHER PROTEST.
SIMPLE MESSAGE, YES. BUT TO A HUNGRY TIGER...
WHEN HE GAVE THE MESSAGE TO THE TIGER —
ALL RIGHT, I'LL WAIT. BUT IF SHE DOESN'T TURN UP WITH THE COW...
...I'LL EAT YOU INSTEAD.
WHAT!
AS YOU KNOW, I'M NOT PARTICULAR ABOUT THE ANIMAL.

FORTUNATELY FOR SHER-SINGH HIS WIFE DID TURN UP—BUT DRESSED AS A MAN, AND BRANDISHING A SICKLE!
I HOPE I FIND A TIGER TODAY TOO!
?!
MM... THE TIGER I HAD FOR BREAKFAST YESTERDAY WAS SO TASTY!
WHAT!
AH! I'M LUCKY! A TIGER!
NO!
HELP!

AMAR CHITRA KATHA

Panel 1:
"MY LORD! WHY ARE YOU RUNNING AWAY?"

Panel 2:
THE TIGER GASPED FOR BREATH AS HE TOLD THE JACKAL ABOUT THE TIGER-EATER.
"THERE'S NO NEED TO BE FRIGHTENED, MY LORD."
"FOR YOU, MAYBE."

Panel 3:
"THAT MONSTER EATS ONLY TIGERS, NOT JACKALS!"

Panel 4:
"I WONDER WHY HE IS SO PARTICULAR ABOUT THE ANIMAL! WHY CAN'T HE EAT JACKALS?"
"MY LORD, PLEASE LISTEN TO ME."

Panel 5:
"THAT MONSTER COULD ONLY BE THE FARMER'S WIFE."

Panel 6:
"THE FARMER'S WIFE! ARE YOU SURE?"
"YES. I SAW HER FROM UP HERE. IT WAS A WOMAN DRESSED LIKE A MAN."

THE TIGER EATER

DON'T GO WITHOUT YOUR BREAKFAST BECAUSE OF A WOMAN.

I DON'T BELIEVE YOU. THAT MONSTER MIGHT HAVE BRIBED YOU TO LURE ME TO HER.

LET'S GO TOGETHER THEN.

YOU MIGHT TAKE ME THERE AND THEN RUN AWAY.

IF THAT'S WHAT YOU FEAR, LET'S TIE OUR TAILS TOGETHER. THEN I CAN'T RUN AWAY.

THE TIGER AGREED. WITH THEIR TAILS TIED TOGETHER THE TWO SET OFF.

MEANWHILE AT THE FIELD —
HA HA! EVERY TIME I THINK OF THAT STUPID ANIMAL I FEEL LIKE LAUGHING.
HO HO HO HO
HO...AH...AH...
NOW WHAT'S THE MATTER?
THE TIGER! THE TIGER IS BACK! LET'S RUN AWAY!
WHAT'S THAT JACKAL DOING WITH HIM? WAIT!
SHE WALKED UP TO THEM.
THANK YOU, FRIEND JACKAL. IT WAS KIND OF YOU TO BRING ME SUCH A FINE, FAT TIGER!

THE TIGER EATER

"I'll finish my share first. Then you can have yours."

Without a moment's delay the tiger turned...

...and fled.

"My lord... my lord!"

The tiger was so frightened that he could hardly hear the jackal. He ran away dragging the poor creature behind him.

HOHO! HA HA!

"That tiger won't ever come here again!"

THE BEAR COMES TO DINNER
MUKHIA, GET ME SOME FIREWOOD!
MUKHIA!
O MUKHIA!
HM!
ZZZZZ
MUKHIA!
EHH...
WHAT ARE YOU DOING?
I AM BUSY... VERY BUSY...
... PRAYING.
PRAYING?

YES, PRAYING! FOR A STORM.
CAN YOU SEE THAT TREE LADEN WITH PEARS?
DO YOU REMEMBER WHAT OUR KIND NEIGHBOUR SAID? ALL PEARS WHICH FALL INTO OUR COURTYARD ARE OURS.
HOW CAN THE FRUIT FALL UNLESS THERE IS A STORM?
BUT, MUKHIA...
WHY DON'T YOU JOIN ME AND PRAY FOR ONE?
WHO WILL MAKE THE KHICHRI THEN?
ARE YOU MAKING KHICHRI?

LET ME NOT STOP YOU THEN. YOU DO YOUR WORK, I'LL DO MINE.
THEN DO IT.
GO TO THE FOREST AND GET SOME WOOD.
WHO? ME? I'M SORRY, I CAN'T.
WHAT IF THE STORM BREAKS OUT WHEN I'M NOT HERE?
THE WOMAN KNEW IT WAS USELESS ARGUING WITH MUKHIA. SHE WENT OUT HERSELF...
...AND RETURNED WITH SOME WOOD.
SHH... PLACE THE BUNDLE DOWN, DON'T DROP IT. YOU'LL SCARE THE SQUIRREL AWAY.

THE TIGER EATER

THE LITTLE RASCAL IS NIBBLING AT A PEAR. HE'LL DROP IT ANY...

CRASH

SEE WHAT YOU'VE DONE! THE SQUIRREL HAS GONE AND...

SHE'S UPSET!

NEVER MIND! I'LL GIVE HER A RIPE PEAR WHEN I GET ONE.

THAT WILL CHEER HER UP.

WHY DO THOSE PEARS HAVE TO CLING TO THE BRANCHES? WHY CAN'T THEY FALL DOWN?	I'M SO-O-O HUNGRY.

SNIFF... SNIFF

SNIFF

SNIFF... SNIFF

SNIFF SNIFF

IT'S YOUR KHICHRI! I KNEW IT.

I COULD TELL BY THE AROMA.

ONLY ONE PERSON IN THE WORLD CAN MAKE KHICHRI THAT HAS SUCH AN AROMA.
NOW!
STOP!
EH?
DON'T TOUCH IT!
YOU WON'T GET EVEN A TINY MORSEL OF IT...
...UNTIL YOU GO TO THE FOREST AND GET SOME WOOD.

YOU WANT ME... TO WORK... ON AN EMPTY STOMACH?
YES. IF YOU WANT THE KHICHRI YOU'LL HAVE TO.
ALL RIGHT.
HERE I GO.
I HATE TO SEND HIM OUT ON AN EMPTY STOMACH...
BUT I'LL HAVE TO... FOR HIS OWN GOOD.
MY DEAR...
WHAT IS IT?
I... ER ...I...

...I WANT TO SNIFF THE KHICHRI JUST ONCE BEFORE I GO.
I WANT TO CARRY ITS AROMA WITH ME. IT WILL ACT AS A TONIC.
ALL RIGHT. YOU MAY SNIFF IT ONCE. BUT JUST ONCE, MIND YOU.
THEN WITH A SMILE ON HIS FACE, MUKHIA WALKED TO THE FOREST.
MM-M-M- IT'S SO GOOD...M-M-M...
WAH! WHAT A KHICHRI!

UNCLE!
EH?
WHERE ARE YOU GOING, UNCLE?
TO THE FOREST, TO GET WOOD.
TO FELL TREES AND GATHER WOOD? YOU'LL HAVE TO WORK VERY HARD.
I DON'T MIND.
YOU DON'T MIND HARD WORK!
NO, NOT AT ALL.
IF I CARRY HOME A BIG BUNDLE OF WOOD, MY WIFE WILL GIVE ME SOME KHICHRI.
KHICHRI?

AND WHAT A KHICHRI ! MM-M -M...
MY FRIEND, I WISH YOU COULD HAVE SMELT IT... MM-M-M.
WILL YOUR WIFE GIVE ME SOME ?
SHE MIGHT.
BUT YOU'LL HAVE TO WORK FOR IT.
LOOK AT ME, ALL SET TO WORK AT MY AGE.
GIVE ME THE AXE, UNCLE ! I WILL GET YOU THE WOOD...
...FOR A SHARE IN THE KHICHRI.
YOU'LL GET ME THE WOOD !

HOW MUCH WILL YOU BRING ?
A LARGE BUNDLE.
I DON'T THINK MY WIFE WILL AGREE. KHICHRI IS AN EXPENSIVE DISH YOU KNOW.
WOULD FOUR HUNDRED KILOS DO ?
MAKE IT FIVE HUNDRED.
THAT'S A LARGE QUANTITY.
THINK OF THE KHICHRI. IT'S A SPECIAL ONE. WE SERVE IT WITH HONEY.
HONEY !
ALL RIGHT ! IT'S A BARGAIN ! YOU GET BACK HOME AND KEEP THE KHICHRI READY...
...I'll COME WITH THE WOOD.

WHEN MUKHIA WENT BACK HOME —
SO YOU ARE BACK EMPTY-HANDED! YOU WON'T...
HAVE PATIENCE, WOMAN, PATIENCE.
MUKHIA TOLD HIS WIFE OF THE BARGAIN HE HAD STRUCK WITH THE BEAR.
YOU WILL BE GETTING FIVE HUNDRED KILOS OF WOOD...
...THANKS TO THE SHREWD BUSINESS SENSE OF YOUR HUSBAND.
OH, YES. YOU HAVE BEEN CLEVER. BUT...
...HAVE YOU TOLD THE BEAR EXACTLY HOW MUCH OF THE KHICHRI HE WILL BE GETTING?
THE BEAR IS A GLUTTON. HE WILL GOBBLE UP ALL THE KHICHRI BEFORE WE HAVE FINISHED OUR FIRST HELPING.

HE EATS FAST. WE EAT SLOWLY. WHAT SHOULD WE DO ?
IT'S SIMPLE. LET'S BEGIN NOW, AND HAVE A FAIR START.
SO THE TWO SAT DOWN TO EAT THE KHICHRI.
AH! IT'S DELICIOUS!
WITH HIS MOUTH FULL OF KHICHRI, MUKHIA REMINDED HIS WIFE OF THE BEAR'S SHARE.
LEAVE SOMETHING FOR THE BEAR.
OF COURSE, WE WILL NOT FORGET OUR GOOD FRIEND.
WE WILL REMEMBER THE POOR BEAR.

CERTAINLY... CERTAINLY.
THUS WHILE THE BEAR WAS BUSY FELLING TREES...
...MUKHIA AND HIS WIFE WERE BUSY DOWNING THE KHICHRI.
WE'LL HAVE TO LEAVE A SHARE FOR THE BEAR...
OF COURSE... A SHARE FOR OUR FRIEND.
!
!
CLANK
CLANK
IT'S OVER! THERE'S NO MORE KHICHRI LEFT IN THE VESSEL.

I KEPT REMINDING YOU NOT TO FORGET THE BEAR.
I CAN'T BLAME YOU. THE KHICHRI WAS VERY TASTY. YET I WISH YOU HADN'T EATEN SO MUCH.
WHAT!
YOU ATE TWICE AS MUCH AS I DID. AND NOW YOU BLAME ME!
ALL RIGHT. ALL RIGHT. I TAKE THE BLAME. BUT WHAT DO WE SAY TO THE BEAR?
THERE HE COMES.
RUN!

THE TIGER EATER

THE WOMAN DRAGGED HER HUSBAND WITH HER.

TO THE ATTIC.

JUST IN TIME! HE'S AT THE DOOR!

AH! THIS IS THE HOUSE. I CAN SEE THE VESSEL OF KHICHRI.

HE THREW DOWN THE LOAD...

...AND WALKED IN.

AH! THE KHICHRI AT LAST!

WHAT!	I'VE BEEN CHEATED!

HE CAUGHT HOLD OF A POST WHICH SUPPORTED THE ROOF AND SHOOK IT WITH ALL HIS MIGHT.

THE ROOF!

SH!

FORTUNATELY THE ROOF HELD.

I'LL TAKE BACK THE WOOD.

BUT HOW CAN I? I'M SO HUNGRY... AND WEAK...

THE TIGER EATER

THE BEAR WENT INTO THE HOUSE AGAIN.

I'LL TAKE THE KHICHRI POT WITH ME AND SMELL IT TILL I FIND SOME FOOD.

LOOK. HE'S GOING OUT...!

SHH...

AS HE CAME OUT OF THE COTTAGE THE BEAR LOOKED UP.

PEARS!

HE TOOK ONE GREAT LEAP...

...AND IN A FEW SECONDS WAS ON THE WALL.

THE NEXT MINUTE HE WAS UP THE TREE.

MM-M-M! DELICIOUS!
LOOK! HE'S EATING ALL OUR PEARS!
SHH...
THE BEAR PAUSED FOR A MOMENT.
WHY I CAN GATHER THESE JUICY PEARS IN THIS VESSEL...
...AND EXCHANGE THEM...
...FOR KHICHRI!
AH! THIS ONE IS NOT YET RIPE. NO ONE WILL ACCEPT IT.

THE TIGER EATER

"Why waste it? I'll eat it up."

"Look at the greedy rascal eating the green ones. He'll be sick."

"Shh..."

"Look. The vessel is full of golden ripe pears... our vessel... our pears..."

"Shh..."

SUDDENLY —

"No... no..."

AHAHA!

29

A H CHE U
A GUNSHOT! I'D BETTER RUN FOR MY LIFE.
HE DROPPED THE VESSEL ...
A H CHE U
... AND BOUNDED AWAY.
WHEN HE WAS OUT OF SIGHT THE COUPLE CAME RUNNING DOWN.
PEARS!
PEARS! JUICY PEARS! OURS AT LAST!

राम ब्रह्म व्यापक जगजाना।
परमानंद परेस पुराना॥

Tulsidas'
Ram Charit Manas

It brought Ramayana to the masses

Read the story in Amar Chitra Katha

SUBSCRIBE NOW!

TINKLE MAGAZINE
FREE* ACK DVD worth ₹149
*with 2 year subscription

1 yr subscription	2 yr subscription
Pay only ~~₹480~~ ₹380!	Pay only ~~₹960~~ ₹750!

TINKLE DIGEST
FREE ACK DVD worth ₹149

1 yr subscription	2 yr subscription
Pay only ~~₹720~~ ₹580!	Pay only ~~₹1440~~ ₹1080!

TINKLE COMBO MAGAZINE + DIGEST
FREE TIME COMPASS DVD worth ₹598

1 yr subscription	2 yr subscription
Pay only ~~₹1200~~ ₹880!	Pay only ~~₹2400~~ ₹1680!

I would like a subscription for

TINKLE MAGAZINE ☐ 1 yr | ☐ 2 yrs
TINKLE COMBO ☐ 1 yr | ☐ 2 yrs
TINKLE DIGEST ☐ 1 yr | ☐ 2 yrs

(Please tick the appropriate box)

YOUR DETAILS*

Name: .... Date of Birth: |__|__| / |__|__| / |__|__|__|__|

Address: ....

.... City: .... Pin: |__|__|__|__|__|__| State: ....

School: .... Class: ....

Tel: .... Mobile: + 91 - |__|__|__|__|__|__|__|__|__|__|

Email: .... Signature: ....

PAYMENT OPTIONS

☐ Cheque /DD:

Please enclose Cheque /DD no. |__|__|__|__|__|__| drawn in favour of 'ACK Media Direct Ltd.'

at .... (bank) for the amount .... ,

dated |__|__| / |__|__| / |__|__|__|__| and send it to: IBH Books & Magazines Distributers Pvt. Ltd., Arch No. 30, West Approach, Below Mahalaxmi Bridge, Mahalaxmi (W), Mumbai - 400034.

☐ Pay Cash on Delivery: Pay cash on delivery of the first issue to the postman. (Additional charge of ₹50 applicable)

☐ Pay by money order: Pay by money order in favour of "ACK Media Direct Ltd."

☐ Online subscription: Please visit: www.amarchitrakatha.com

For any queries or further information: Email: customerservice@ack-media.com or Call: 022-40497435 / 36